The Rape Victim

Sitwala Imenda

Mulindeti Publishers and Distributors

P.O. Box 910055

Mongu

E-mail: imendask@yahoo.com

Mobile: +27 82 888 3606

ISBN 978-0-620-45762-0

Author's Other Books

Better to Lie? Pretoria, Via Africa, 1994.

Republished as: **Unmarried Wife**
East African Educational Publishers: Spear Books,
Nairobi, KENYA, 1996.

The Blairing Kofi Bush War of Iraq – Who was Insane? (Epic Poem), Trafford Publishing, Victoria, Canada, 2004. (Available online).

My Grandfather's God, Mipal Printers and Publishers, Lusaka, Zambia, 2004. (Available online).

Mind Over Matter, Mipal Printers and Publishers, Lusaka, Zambia, 2004. (Available online).

Dancing mice and other African folktales (co-author: LN Inambao), Mipal Printers and Publishers, Lusaka, Zambia, 2004. (Available online).

Imenda, SN. **2014: Zambia's constitution finally righted**, [Novel]. Mulindeti Publishers and Distributors, 2008. (Available online).

Imenda, SN. **University Xenophobia: Real or Imagined?** Kwarts Publishers, Centurion, South Africa. 2017. (Available online).

Imenda, SN. **Silozi-English Dictionary of Common Animals,** Mulindeti Publishers and Distributors, Mongu, 2022.

Imenda, SN (2020). **Dziwani Zacilengedwe: Buku la m'Chinyanja ndi Chingerezi la maina a nyama**

zodziwika, Mulindeti Publishers and Distributors, Mongu, 2022.

Imenda, SN. **Silozi-English Dictionary of Common Birds,** Mulindeti Publishers and Distributors, Mongu, 2023.

Dedication

To all victims of the law

THE RAPE VICTIM

'He who is merely just is severe' -
Voltaire, French writer (1694-1778)

1

A lover who reasons is no lover - Norman Douglas,
English writer (1868-1952).

Members of the general public were divided
over the matter. Most men felt vulnerable and believed
that the outcome of this court case would seal their fate
in ways that would be excessively dangerous, explosive,
volatile, unimaginably brutal unprecedented,
unpredictable or even catastrophic. On the other hand,
the majority of the women felt that the judiciary system
needed to be tough on men like Mr. Sieo Liwetete by
making a clear and unequivocal statement to the rest of
the men folk that rape was a very serious crime, and not
to be made one's lifetime career, pass-time or hobby.
The feelings of the women were reflected in the words
of the prosecutor, Mr. Nchiba Ngweshi, in his
submission that "men need to realise that the days when
they could sexually assault women with impunity are
now over. It is the duty of the courts to make this point
unambiguously clear to all concerned."
    The case between Mrs. Mamunyandi Liwetete
and her husband had drawn a lot of interest, not only
within Zambia, but also from far and beyond. Although
Mr. and Mrs. Liwetete were on separation and no longer

living together they were still legally married. However, because Mr. Liwetete was now living with another woman in Mungu's Yeta compound, somehow Mrs. Liwetete felt that she also could do the same and have the freedom not to let her social life slip away and slide into oblivion at the prime of her years. After all, as they say, "time waits for no one."

"Mr Liwetete, can you tell us exactly what happened on the day in question?" asked the prosecutor, Mr. Ngweshi.

"I had gone to visit my wife and children that evening and found her entertaining another man," Mr. Liwetete replied.

"Then what happened?" the prosecutor pressed on.

"It was late. It must have been 22h00, or thereabouts. When I entered the living room I found a man lying down on the couch with his bald head resting on my wife's lap. Our three children were already asleep in their bedrooms," Mr. Liwetete replied – trying to squeeze in as much detail as possible, as if to save the precious time of the court.

"Did you recognise the man you found resting his head on your wife's lap?" the prosecutor wanted to know, also rubbing in the thing about the man resting his head on the lap of someone else's wife.

"Yes, I did. The man had been known to me for a long time, since our childhood days – as a matter of fact. We had been very close friends for a long time, even during the many years I was in prison. He visited me regularly, and I never imagined that he would be the first person to take advantage of the domestic problems I was having with my wife at the time. Now, it would even appear that he may have been at the centre of those problems."

"Did you say you were once in prison?"

"Yes, my Lord, for a long time – and I am still very bitter about it."

"Can you tell us why you were in prison...."

"Objection, my Lord, could my learned colleague restrict himself to the present case!" objected Mr. Liwetete's attorney, Mrs. Ngw'elele Lubango.

Mrs. Lubango was a well known and respected attorney, especially in civil and criminal cases involving marital conflicts and other passion-related offences. Mr. Liwetete also felt that being defended by a female attorney, who would inevitably have to show both empathy and sympathy with his position, would stand him a good chance of getting a fairer and better-balanced hearing than if defended by a fellow male attorney. In addition, he felt that, as a result of such kind consideration of his position by a member of the fairer sex, public opinion would also sway in his favour. "In sensitive matters involving high emotions like this one, as opposed to matters which are purely of logic, one cannot rule out the power and influence of public opinion," Mr. Liwetete had comforted himself.

"Sustained!" the Honourable Judge Mulumesi ruled.

Mr. Liwetete had had a previous conviction of rape and spent nine years in jail. At the time of his conviction, it was widely believed that the sentence had been too harsh, given the uncertainty of the facts put before the court, and that he was a first offender. However, as in the present case, it had been a case of public opinion and the courts pushing for a firm stand on gender-based violence, particularly rape.

The sentence had shocked not only Mr. Liwetete but most of his friends, who had known him to be a gentle and caring person, who would not even squash a mosquito feasting on his sweet blood to protect himself from contracting malaria.

Mr. Liwetete's life had started pretty much like all other people's: eventful but normal. He had attended Christian schools where he learnt the commandments and the importance of being a good citizen. He endeavoured to abide by rules and the law at all times and in all circumstances. Even after leaving high school, he had managed to follow Christian standards of life and all other associated values. However, all hell had broken loose soon after leaving university. He graduated as a mathematics teacher and was posted to a rural school, St. Michael's, in the Sikongo area of Kalabo.

However, as fate would have it, a few weeks after his arrival at the school he was attacked by common influenza; his nose was burning and he was nursing a very high temperature. In accordance with school regulations Mr. Liwetete sought and obtained permission from the principal to go to the local hospital, which was five kilometres away from the school. There was no regular public transportation system in this rural area between the school and the hospital, so he borrowed the school bicycle which was normally used by the school messenger on his many errands which he had to make in order to keep the school in touch with other institutions and government departments. To get to the hospital from the school one needed to negotiate two hills, separated by a valley. By the time Mr. Liwetete got to the hospital he felt extremely tired and weak. He was sweating profusely. He sat down under a tree outside the out-patient building for a brief moment, to catch his breath and recuperate.

After a little while, Mr. Liwetete felt sufficiently cooled down and well-collected to proceed to the registration office for a hospital card. He was subsequently led to see the clinical officer for the initial screening, for, only seriously ill patients, as judged by this person, were referred to the medical officer. His eyes looked pale and tired. He complained of a headache and fever to the clinical officer. He was then sent to Room 4 to have his temperature and other things checked by the nurse.

"Hey, lady, don't we know each other?" Mr. Liwetete asked as he entered the room.

"Of course we know each other, are you not Mr. Liwetete, or should I call you Sieo?" the nurse replied, reminding Mr. Liwetete of his childhood name. She continued, "In fact, I already heard about your coming to the high school. One of these days I was going to come and look you up. My younger sister needs a school place for next year, and I thought maybe you might be in a position to help," nurse Nakatenge replied.

Nakatenge was a beautiful young lady who caught Mr. Liwetete's attention many years back. Mr. Liwetete and Nakatenge used to stay in the same residential area at Sancta Maria Mission, Lukulu, whenever Mr. Liwetete used to go and visit his elder sister during school holidays. Mr. Liwetete's elder sister used to work with Nakatenge's elder brother at the Mission hospital. At that time, Mr. Liwetete attended high school at St John's College in Mungu, and stayed in boarding during term time.

Although Mr. Liwetete's holiday visits to Lukulu were for the most part brief the beauty of this young girl, with an ebony complexion, always made him involuntarily salivate at her sight. He always wished that he got to know her better. But she was too young then, and Mr. Liwetete had a big job of fighting back his mind's tendency to get carried away. He knew he had to fast for quite a while yet before the food would be ready for consumption. At the time he was also greatly assisted by his faith. He would pray each time he felt being tempted by the evil one and rebuked Satan for daring to implant his wicked and dirty thoughts into his holy and innocent mind.

Now, Nakatenge was a mature lady, and still looking fresh and pretty. There are women whose touch of beauty evades them as years roll by – not so with Nakatenge. The white nurses' uniform she was wearing was immaculately clean and made her glitter like an angel in paradise. For a moment Mr. Liwetete was mesmerised by the unchanging beauty of this young lady and even forgot why he was in Room 4 at the hospital.

"Oh, yes. You are welcome to visit me any time of day or night. If I can be of any assistance to your sister I'll be pleased to help. In fact, I would even plead with the principal to take her in; as a matter of fact, I'd literally go down on my knees should this be necessary. My house is Number 6 in the teachers' compound," Mr. Liwetete heard his disobedient tongue blurt out unnecessary details in response to Nakatenge's simple request. Many thoughts raced through his head as he looked her over – as if she were a specimen in a biology laboratory. Silently, his mind began to glorify this flower of the heavens and earth:

Am I – or am I not

Abundantly blessed
To be in this room
At this time
Am I dreaming
Or am I awake
The African woman
Elegant at all times
Time and space
Timeless beauty
Her figure filling the space
Of her attire
Special at all times

The African woman
At all times elegant as eland
Timeless beauty
Body parts wholly in proportion
Body parts perfectly joined
Indeed well connected
The behind is well rounded
And gingerly
As if filled with jelly
Tasty like ginger beer
Men wake up in the morning
After a night of moaning
And for ever left mourning
And yearning for more

African woman
Her long dark legs shining like silver
When the sun sits on them
The lovely beads around her waist
Hidden inside her skirt
Made from animal skin

Dark as ebony
All parts in harmony
Not bony
Sweet as honey
Salt of my food
Sugar for my tea
Spicy and tender
No need for meat tenderiser
Naturally African
African woman
There is no other like her

Oh, Yes!
Black woman of Africa
Black as ebony
Tall as cypress
Elegant as eland
Naturally beautiful
Beautifully natural
Full of grace and style
Pleasing to the eye
Charismatic and charming
Attractive and entrancing
Captivating and enticing
Fascinating and tempting
Inviting and inveigling
Magnetic and enigmatic

Oh, Yes!
Black woman of Africa
Black as ebony
Tall as cypress
Elegant as eland
What else can one say?

"By the way, can I have your card, what is troubling you today?" Nakatenge enquired, realising that her visitor had taken leave of his consciousness, and was in deep slumber. She took Mr. Liwetete's card and politely asked him to remove his shoes and step on the scale to have his weight measured.

Although he did not see the need for someone with a running nose to have his weight measured Mr. Liwetete, nonetheless, obliged. He was also glad that he was wearing his good socks on this very important day - not his other pair which showed his heel and some of his toes. His weight was measured, followed by his height; then he was instructed to open his mouth and lift his tongue to allow the thermometer to be placed below it. He shut his mouth and after a little while the temperature was read off; it was 40^0c. His blood pressure was slightly high, but not frightening.

With this information Mr. Liwetete was now ready to go back to the clinical officer for a diagnosis.

"I'll come and check on you this afternoon when I knock off to see how you are doing. Your temperature is rather high," Nakatenge quipped as Mr. Liwetete was leaving the room.

"Sure, you are welcome, any time," Mr. Liwetete was just too keen for such a visit, despite being temporarily decimated by the elements.

Later that afternoon Nakatenge and her friend, Nembele, went to visit Mr. Liwetete at his house in the teachers' compound. Nakatenge had changed from her white uniforms into ordinary clothing. She dressed simple but looked natural, immaculate and dignified. There was no doubt that Nakatenge was excessively attractive. Anyone who has not yet met Nakatenge has not yet seen a truly beautiful African woman.

After Nakatenge and Nembele had been let into the living room by Mr. Liwetete's domestic helper, Mushuna, Mr. Liwetete was informed of their presence.

"There are two ladies here to see you, sir," Mushuna reported after knocking and entering Mr. Liwetete's bedroom.

"Ask them to come into the bedroom and bring two table chairs for them to sit on," he directed.

Mr. Liwetete lay in his very simple and ordinary bed, trying as much as possible to obey the clinical officer's orders to stay in bed and have as much rest as possible, as a central piece of his treatment regime.

"How are you feeling now, you look terrible?" Nakatenge enquired rather rhetorically after the usual formalities had been dispensed with.

"I am feeling much better, thank you. It's just the heat, I think."

Nakatenge leaned forward and touched Mr. Liwetete's forehead with the back of her hand to feel his temperature. Her touch sent a sizzling sensation throughout Mr. Liwetete's body. He felt electricity racing through his entire body mass, touching every vein and joint – pleasantly though, like one who has just undergone divine healing.

"Your temperature feels normal. I am sure you'll be feeling much better by tomorrow. Mr Liwetete, meet my friend Nembele. We work together at the hospital," Nakatenge introduced her friend – and turning to Nembele, she continued, "I have known this gentleman for quite a while now. He is what I would call my 'home boy' although I do not really know where his traditional home is. I felt very happy to hear that he had come to work at this school. He reminds me of my good old days at Sancta Maria Mission; in fact, seeing him here reminds me of my childhood."

Nembele was of medium build, and a little lighter skinned than Nakatenge. She was also beautiful and attractive in her own unique way, but not as nearly pretty as Nakatenge was. Her physical features were somewhat different from Nakatenge's but still, no man would look at her only once. She was a local girl and had earlier attended the same high school at which Mr. Liwetete was now teaching.

Later on that afternoon, Mr. Liwetete's two esteemed visitors prepared supper for him and insisted on him eating at least some of it before they left. He felt so honoured and blessed that he wished this was what the clinical officer had ordered.

After they had left, Mr. Liwetete started to imagine how nice it would be to have a woman of Nakatenge's general profile and stature in his house as a wife, for the rest of his life. Now that he was a working young man he did not see any reason why such a wish could not be made to materialise. Besides, he knew Nakatenge to be a girl of substance - a girl he had felt attracted to ever since the very first day he set his eyes upon her – but a girl, nonetheless, hiding behind some kind of mystique.

True to Nakatenge's word, Mr. Liwetete felt much better the following morning. However, he decided to stay home – more for the purpose of obeying the hospital's orders than for the need to do so.

When Nakatenge and Nembele came to visit him later that next day they found him feeling much better. He was teaching Mushuna how to play chess. These two beautiful young ladies had no idea about chess and soon Mr. Liwetete was deep into teaching them the moves and rules of the game. However, despite Mr. Liwetete's good teaching skills only Nembele appeared to be making some progress. On her part, Nakatenge was either hard of hearing or she was just absent-minded and lost in thought, for some reason or other. After some time, Mr. Liwetete realised that the latter was most probably the case. She was miles away from the game of chess he was trying so hard to shove down her throat. "She is probably in love," Mr. Liwetete silently massaged his own ego.

The two ladies later left and, by that time, Mr. Liwetete had already made up his mind, "Nakatenge is the girl I must get married to – or no girl at all."

The following day at work Mr. Liwetete felt anxious at the way time appeared to be mark-timing. He had already decided that he should pay Nakatenge a visit after school, either at the hospital or at her house. This, he later did and a very strong, romantic relationship soon evolved between the two of them – and not very long thereafter plans for marriage were afoot.

However, while marriage arrangements were still in progress, Nakatenge had to go away to Lusaka on a short course in psychiatric nursing. It was as a result of this move that Mr. Liwetete's destiny later took a sour turn. Nembele continued to visit him in Nakatenge's absence, sometimes at really odd and awkward hours late at night, until one day the inevitable happened. On this particular day, Nembele came to visit Mr. Liwetete at about 21h00 as he was about to go to bed, and soon it started to rain heavily and incessantly. The rain continued pouring down for a long time - until fate drove the two young and hot-blooded individuals to the conclusion that it was not going to be possible for Nembele to go back to her house; that she should stay the night. In the interactions which ensued they finally ended up sharing the same bed ostensibly as a temporary, stop-gap measure to take care of each other's physiological needs. As fate would have it though, this gentleman's agreement, a friendship of convenience, between Mr. Liwetete and Nembele marked the start of a down-hill spiral for Mr. Liwetete.

<u>2</u>

If a woman once makes up her mind to marry a man, nothing but instant flight can save him - W. Somerset Maugham, English writer (1874-1965).

One day, Nembele was gently stroking the hair on Mr. Liwetete's chest, in a really romantic atmosphere as they slept together, when she suddenly came up with a rather awkward question, "Mr. Liwetete, darling, do you really love me?"

The issue of whether or not there was love between the two of them had never before been a topic of discussion. From the time their intimate relationship started up until this day, they appeared to be bonded to one another more by forces of their circumstances than by this thing called 'love'. So, this question took Mr. Liwetete totally by surprise. Clearly, he needed time to digest the question and give a well-considered answer; a spontaneous answer was not the route to take. But his friend appeared not to have much time; she needed a more spontaneous answer than a calculated response. "Don't tell me you have just been using me to fill up boring time and space left by Nakatenge's departure?" Nembele asked.

The pressure building in Mr. Liwetete's chest was not good for his health. He reflected briefly on Nembele's question, but sensed danger; he realised that the problem was not whether or not he loved Nembele. He was extremely worried by what lay behind the question. In retrospect, he surmised that he had most probably been too naïve not to have expected this question to have come sooner, rather than later.

"Nembele, you are a very pretty woman. Every man would fall in love with you instantly, at first sight. No man would look at you only once," Mr. Liwetete replied rather superficially and small-mindedly, skirting the gist of Nembele's enquiry; he was in some kind of fix.

"But, have you fallen in love with me yourself – instantly, at first sight?" she insisted on a less philosophical answer.

It dawned on Mr. Liwetete that he had actually never before told her that he loved her. It had never before been necessary to say so, or not to say so. On her part, perhaps for the same reasons – whatever those reasons may have been, she also had never told Mr. Liwetete that she loved him.

"Of course, I do like you very much," Mr. Liwetete answered feeling cornered and quite uneasy.

"What about love, do you love me?"

"Look at all this time we have been spending together, do you think I'd be spending all this time with someone I did not love?"

"Well, if you do, I would like you to seriously think about the future and happiness of your child that I am carrying. I want you to realise how difficult it is for a single mother to bring up a child alone, and how confusing it would be for the child not to have both parents at home," Nembele motivated her case as much as possible.

Mr. Liwetete began to catch Nembele's drift. This is what he had feared. It was only a few days previously that Nembele had told him about the pregnancy. As things were, Mr. Liwetete was still digesting the matter – and catching quite a great deal of constipation in the process. To start with, he was not even sure whether or not she was really pregnant, or she was merely trying to exact some form of serious commitment from him – such as a marriage, through false pretences. He was still trying to get to grips with this problem in order to work out the best strategy for dealing with it. He was having sleepless nights, particularly since his love for Nakatenge had not waned in any way. Furthermore, he could not understand how such a well-informed nurse, with all types of contraceptives and other measures at her disposal, could so easily have fallen pregnant.

Mr. Liwetete was gentle in his demeanour and character, but on this occasion, he wondered whether being a bit wild in his approach wouldn't be a better thing to do. He was really choking and running short of breath. Which ever way he thought about the matter, he couldn't help but blame Nembele one-hundred percent for making herself fall pregnant – if at all she was.

"Alright, dear. You did well to bring the matter up, I'll think about it," Mr. Liwetete replied, wishing to cut the conversation short by deferring the crunch to another time. He was feeling sleepy and somewhat tired after they had made love.

"Do you mean you have not been thinking about it since I told you the other day that I was carrying your baby?" Nembele refused to be shut out.

"I've been thinking about it, day and night, but so far I have not been able to see my way clear. You know the relationship I have with your best friend and how far we have gone in preparing for our marriage..."

"That's all you think about, all the time, eeh? It is Nakatenge all the time, what about me and my feelings? Do you ever stop to think about my feelings and self respect? How do you think I'll feel when I deliver your baby and everyone in this community knows it is yours, but you are married to someone who used to be my best friend...?"

Mr. Liwetete could not remember how many questions he was expected to answer in one and the same breath but, somehow, he knew that things were bad. Her voice was rising with every question that she asked. He thought of reminding her that if she had not been visiting him for long hours and, more often than not, at odd times, she would most probably not be in the kind of situation she now found herself – assuming that she was indeed pregnant. However, on second thoughts he decided against this confrontational approach. He just decided to keep quiet and absorb whatever was coming his way, particularly considering that Nembele had rejected his earlier, off-the-cuff, suggestion about an abortion when the news was first broken to him. Somehow, she had appeared to regard the matter of her pregnancy in some positive light – and, consequently, argued in a matter-of-fact way that an action such as an abortion would go against the will of God - the Almighty, and would send both of us to a place of everlasting anguish called hell. When she took this moralistic stance, Mr. Liwetete had decided not to play the devil by insisting on a worldly solution against what would be the will of society's moral majority. He felt morally obliged to respect Nembele's position - at least on face value and for the moment. He was, however, troubled by the illogical nature of the heavenly argument that kicked in only to redeem the pregnancy when the actions that led to the pregnancy were, themselves, equally immoral but remained unchallenged. He wondered to himself, "Were we both not already on our way to hell, anyway, even if there had been no pregnancy?"

For now, Mr. Liwetete remembered that Nakatenge's auntie and uncle were arriving the following day to discuss lobola and work out other details relating to the marriage. Nembele knew all about this and somehow it made her feel very insecure and anxious. There had also been an understanding - a gentleman's agreement which they had arrived at on the fateful rainy day, to the effect that once Mr. Liwetete got married to Nakatenge they would stop seeing each other. It seemed all these issues and arrangements were putting pressure on Nembele and her true feelings and colours were now bubbling to the surface. The pregnancy, real or contrived, was undoubtedly a major contributor in this regard. Mr. Liwetete had also known that bringing Nakatenge's name into this discussion, albeit inevitably so, would complicate the discussion beyond reason - and so it did.

"Why don't we stop this discussion and pick it up some other time when our minds are clearer and our temperaments are sober?" Mr. Liwetete endeavoured to bargain for a little space to allow a little reason to prevail over the situation. Unfortunately, his friend was not in any position for interim arrangements and compromises which would merely postpone her search for a lasting solution to her quagmire – thereby prolonging her anguish and grief.

So, in one instant, she had turned the warm ambiance of love that glowed between herself and Mr. Liwetete, as they spent their last night together before Nakatenge's return, into raging flames of jealousy – unstoppable by any means. She wanted to know where she stood right there and then. Besides, with the arrival of Nakatenge and her parents the following day, her future looked dim indeed.

"Why don't you want to discuss it now? Are you waiting for Nakatenge's permission? There may be a lot at stake for you in your proposed marriage to your queen but to me it doesn't mean anything. Do you understand? All I want is for you to be man enough and tell me what you'll do with me and your baby," Nembele retorted.

She started to scream about how Mr. Liwetete had just been using her to quench his libido owing to Nakatenge's stupid sanctions. Nakatenge had refused Mr. Liwetete any sexual pleasures until after marriage. Nembele was really frantic and was threatening that she would 'show' Mr. Liwetete a thing or two, if he wasn't careful.

Mr. Liwetete tried to calm her down, "Please, lower your voice and let's discuss this matter without raising hell for the neighbours!" However, the more he tried to intervene the worse it became. He left the bedroom and went to the toilet, but Nembele followed him and kept on banging on the toilet door. The noise was too much. He opened the door to get out of the toilet, but no sooner had he done so, than Nembele went for his throat at the first opportunity and started throttling and chocking him. He held her hands and disengaged them in a bid to salvage his throat. He managed to do so and pushed her away. Once free, she sprung to his face and scratched him with her sharp fingernails. He pushed her again and shouted, "I'll beat you up if you try to touch me again, do you hear me?"

"Beat me! Beat me if you are a real man!" She screamed back.

Mr. Liwetete looked at her briefly, shook his head in a mixture of disbelief, dismay and anger before making a turn for his bedroom.

Nembele jumped on top of him again; he shook her off somewhat violently and she fell to the concrete floor with a thud – it must have hurt a bit because she sat there for a moment. At last, Mr. Liwetete had a bit of time and space to go into his bedroom. He locked the door soon after he was inside, while Nembele was still struggling to gather herself up. She was wearing only her black half-slip petticoat. She had her underwear rolled up her left arm in order to free her hands for a good fight. Almost as soon as he had entered the bedroom he heard her unlock the back door and then heard her footsteps fading away into the dark night. At this stage Mr. Liwetete was really fed-up and was only too happy to be back in his bedroom. He did not want to see her again in his life, ever, and didn't care how she went home without her clothes; neither did he care about his baby she was purportedly carrying. For now, it just felt like good riddance.

All the while, Mushuna kept to his room, which was only next door to Mr. Liwetete's. Being a well-mannered young man from the rural areas that he was, he did not want to over-step the line and poke his nose in matters that were outside his league. He knew that quarrels and disagreements occurred between couples – officially married or otherwise. So, it would have been out of place for him to intervene at any stage during the fracas, although he followed most of the ugly confrontation from earshot. In any case, at the time when the fracas was taking place outside Mr. Liwetete's bedroom, he wasn't quite sure if the contenders in this fight were properly dressed or not. He dared not venture out of his room with the prospect of feasting his eyes upon the unimaginable.

"How did this all start?" Mr. Liwetete asked himself, once in the comfort of his bedroom. There was nothing that came to his mind to justify why an evening which had started off so romantically and peaceful should have ended up in such hostility, animosity and bitterness. For now, the only thing he wanted was to sleep and get this whole fiasco behind him – and out of his mind. He was feeling itchy on the face because of the scratches occasioned by Nembele's sharp fingernails. He thought of going to wash his face off but decided against it. He was too tired.

"Let me just take a nice warm bath in the morning so that Nakatenge and her parents find me fresh and ready," he advised himself.

On his part, because his parents' home was far from Sikongo, he had organised a few 'uncles' locally – some senior teachers to stand for him in the lobola negotiations. Soon afterwards, he drifted into sleep.

"Police! Open!" came shouts and rough knocks on Mr. Liwetete's bedroom door. First, these loud bangs and voices sounded distant and faint, as if in a dream. However, it was not long before Mr. Liwetete realised that the loud knocks were not in his imagination but were real. He put on his trousers with trembling hands.

He was feeling sleepy, upset and irritable. No one had bothered to lock the back door after Nembele had stormed out. After all, there were no professional thieves and criminals in this sleepy rural area. Casual thieves would always be caught, and they were all well known.

"What is going on?" He asked as soon as he opened his bedroom door.

"Come, we are going together to the police station," one policeman said and led him away roughly. A second policeman entered the bedroom and collected all female clothing from there, as evidence.

"What, to the police station for what?" Mr. Liwetete shouted back. However, before he realised it, he was already in handcuffs and being escorted outside.

When they got outside, he realised that the house was surrounded by policemen. He was lifted up and literally thrown into the back of a waiting police vehicle like a bag of charcoal. He fell with a thud onto the hard surface of the vehicle – slightly sliding forward. Mushuna was also shoved onto the back of the police pick-up van, but it was much better for him because he wasn't hand-cuffed. His name had also come up in Nembele's rumblings at the police station. The police pick-up van had an ugly looking canopy, as they always do – which was then securely locked from outside once the cargo had been loaded. Two policemen guarded them while the driver sped off to the police station as if he was late by two days.

Many things raced through Mr. Liwetete's mind but none of them could explain the treatment he was now receiving at the hands of these ill-mannered policemen. Nothing could explain why he was bundled out of his house in such a hurry, without even being given a chance to put on his shirt or shoes. Nor could anything explain why he had to be hand-cuffed and slapped repeatedly by policemen, who were supposed to protect innocent people like him from criminals.

Soon, they were at the police station, where upon he was bundled out of the police pick-up van in the same rough manner as he had earlier been helped into it. He was instructed to sit on the floor in one corner of the Charge Office behind the counter and told to wait there. He was now feeling really itchy on the face. The slaps which he had received from Constable Ndikusi, in particular, placed as cherry on top of the scratches which Nembele had earlier administered to his face, were now taking their toll. He thought of laying charges against Constable Ndikusi – but then how would anyone distinguish between the damage earlier administered by Nembele and the cherry planted by Constable Ndikusi on top of Nembele's damage? Mr. Liwetete resolved that laying charges would complicate his predicament even further. Mushuna was directed to sit on the floor behind the reception counter, next to his master.

After what appeared to be an eternity of waiting in wonderment, Nembele entered the Charge Office, escorted by two police officers one male and one female. Rape charges were laid against Mr. Liwetete, and since Nembele had torn her underwear and petticoat on her way to the police station - plus the fact that some of her clothes were found in Mr. Liwetete's bedroom, on top of forensic evidence from the hospital, there was overwhelming evidence to convict him. The evidence provided by Mushuna, although fully complementary to Mr. Liwetete's account of the events of that day, did not in any way help Mr. Liwetete's case. Society had to be protected from people of Mr. Liwetete's kind. That was how he had earned the nine-year jail term - ostensibly to deter him, and others like him, from laying their soiled hands-on innocent women and committing the same despicable act of violence against the fairer sex in future. This rather harsh sentence, meted against someone who had not even committed the offence, was in line with what the 'fortune teller' had told Mr. Liwetete the day before sentencing.

What had happened was that Mr. Liwetete's friend by the name of Singongi had heard of a fortune teller, and persuaded Mr. Liwetete to go and consult her the day before judgment.

"This lady is really good," Singongi had explained. "She has helped many people. She is a palm reader. All she needs is just a few minutes to study the lines of your palm and then she tells you everything about your life – past, present and future. She is really gifted."

However, even after this explanation, Mr. Liwetete was still not clear how seeing her would be of any use.

"What happens after she has told me everything about my past and present – which I already know anyway, and then goes further and tells me that I am going to jail?" Mr. Liwetete had wanted to know from his friend.

"Then we ask her if she can give us something to stop you from going to jail. You see, it is better for us to go and see her now because after you have been sent to jail, there is nothing we can do at that stage. I offer to pay the consultation fee."

This was how they ended up going to see the lady. Indeed, it just took her a few minutes to tell them that Mr. Liwetete was a rather unfortunate individual who would go through periods of darkness – brought about by circumstances beyond his control. These episodes of darkness would, luckily, be punctuated by some happy events in between.

Apart from the generality of the palm-reader's statements, Mr. Liwetete still had problems interpreting what she was really referring to. "Doesn't everyone have periods of darkness and episodes of joy, anyway?" he wondered. He wondered why a 'fortune teller' should also tell someone about his or her misfortunes.

As it turned out, the next day he was handed a nine-year jail term – with no portion of it suspended; neither was there an option for a fine or any form of community-based punishment. It just looked like seeing the fortune teller had done nothing but hype up the brutality of the judge in his quest to turn him into an exemplar of the cruelty of courts – under the noble guise of meting out sentences which were meant to deter those who would have committed the same offence in future. In the sadistic and narcissistic mind of the judge, it had appeared that he was bent on ensuring that every time a rape case was heard in his court, the sentence must be scaled up. So, the period of darkness for Mr. Liwetete had started.

After he came out of jail, seven years ago, he managed put his life back on track by starting up a food-supply business. This came about, courtesy of an honest crook who made it possible for him to earn a sizeable amount of cash upon his release. The cash had been handed over to him on the same day of his release from prison as payment for his part in a crime that he hardly knew anything about.

The honest crook happened to be a senior warder who ran a gang of armed robbers from prison. Mr.

Liwetete was lucky to have gone to jail with a driving skill which he was asked to utilise about three weeks before his scheduled release. The driver of the senior warder's gang had suddenly been assailed by a very aggressive stomach bug on the evening the gang had a very big 'operation' to carry out. The gang member's stomach was biting and running non-stop; he suffered from a cholera-like diarrhoea. On the other hand, all the groundwork for this 'operation' had been done, and there was no question of a postponement, rescheduling or anything of that sort. For a reason that Mr. Liwetete will never know or understand, he had been roped into this 'operation' at the eleventh hour. The only brief he received was that he would drive military-style, and that this was a very sensitive 'operation' with absolutely no margin for error. Throughout the exercise, he would receive instructions from the senior warder, who would be sitting next to him in the front passenger seat. From then on, things moved too quickly for Mr. Liwetete's judicious recollection. After they were safely back on prison grounds, Mr. Liwetete had been kept behind by the warder for a debriefing. "You listen to me very carefully and attentively because I am not going to repeat myself", the senior warder had started his debriefing in a matter-of-fact way – actually, more like a stern warning. "What happens here today remains inside your head up to the time you die, do you understand me? Actually, nothing happened today; you did nothing, and you saw nothing – do you hear what I am saying?"

Not that Mr. Liwetete had much to say on the matter. He just stared at the senior warder as if he were a zombie. "Thank you very much for your courage and good driving. You must have been a taxi driver before you came to prison. This was a very successful operation, and for your troubles, you have earned yourself enough money to start a decent life for yourself when you walk out of this place in a few weeks' time. Do you hear what I am saying? Since you're leaving the prison shortly, this will compensate you for the many years you stayed here. You should be grateful because even your friends who stayed behind when you came to jail will not have this kind of money in their bank accounts, if at all they even have bank accounts. I should hear nothing about this. It is a secret you'll take with you to your grave; any word about it, and you'll just disappear – juts like that!" the warder concluded with a snapping of fingers, producing a sharp clicking sound.

On the day of his release, the senior warder had directed him to a street corner in town where an unknown man, wearing a baseball cap which almost completely hid his eyes, thrust a money bag into his bosom and quickly disappeared. He was later to find out that the money bag contained an equivalent of US$150 000 hard, cold cash, in local currency. It was both sweet and scary – the sweet part was the money, but how could someone you've never met give you so much money? It was really scary that someone in the underworld knew him, but he had no idea who the fellow was. It showed him that some crooks could be honest, indeed.

Everything, notwithstanding, he leaned on this money and steadied himself quite comfortably after his released. He started a food supply business, first supplying the same prison where he had been held – and subsequently supplying hospitals and other institutions. It wasn't long before he had established himself as a businessman of note.

Soon after he was firmly on his feet, he got married to Mamunyandi and started raising a family. They now have three children, and he has never been able to trace either Nembele or Nakatenge ever since his release from jail. Perhaps they were deliberately hiding away from him, not wanting to associate with a jail-bird - a rapist at that. As such, he had not been able to establish the authenticity of Nembele's pregnancy, which had led to his incarceration for nine years. If there had been a child, perhaps they were shielding him or her from knowing the 'truth' about his or her father – that he was a convicted rapist. However, what was still vivid in Mr. Liwetete's mind was the huge scale of the scandal which filled the entire small settlement of Sikongo and the neighbouring villages the day Nakatenge and her parents arrived to find that he was in police custody on a charge of raping Nakatenge's best friend. Nakatenge had been deeply disappointed, although she had been ably comforted by her caring and loving auntie. Her uncle was somewhat untouched by the whole fiasco and found the whole episode somewhat amusing. "This is really a he-man; a man and a half – one who knows what to do with a careless woman when he sees one!" he had teased his niece. And he had hastened to add that there was more to the story than what was known at the time. He had supported his suspicions by opining that he did not understand how rape charges could be preferred against a man sleeping peacefully in his house late at night. By the same token, he did not understand what the woman was doing in Mr. Liwetete's bedroom deep into the night, unless she had been held there against her will – but nobody had said that this had been the case. "If Mr. Liwetete was caught in the lady's house at that late hour, then I would understand that this man had trespassed and violated the woman's privacy and dignity – in which case he would have brought this upon himself. However, until someone tells me what this beautiful, self-respecting young lady was looking for in Mr. Liwetete's house at that ungodly hour, I'll still hold the view that rape is out of the question. Where I come from, in my village, the young lady would be the one faced with difficult questions to answer," he had surmised.

However, Nakatenge was too distraught, at the time, to delve into the whole story, and took the position that the less she knew about it the better for her soul and peace of mind.

Despite the normal life that Mr. Liwetete had endeavoured to lead ever since he was released from jail, things started going sour in his marriage nine or so months ago, leading to his present unofficial separation from his family. Ironically, he was now again facing rape charges which could see him back in jail – this time for a very long time as a habitual offender.

"I apologise, my Lord," the prosecutor, Mr Ngweshi replied after being ruled out of order by Judge Mulumesi. He continued with Mr. Liwetete's cross examination, "Mr Liwetete, you have not yet told us in full what actually happened that evening when you visited my client and allegedly found her entertaining your childhood friend?"

"Well, as soon as my wife saw me, she pushed her friend away from her lap and rushed to our bedroom for cover. I ran after her in order to bring her back to the living room to explain what was going on."

"Then what happened? Did you manage to bring her back?"

"It took a little while. She locked the bedroom door, and it took a lot of pep talk to persuade her to unlock it. By the time we both got back to the living room her companion had fled."

"Was it at this stage that you started beating my client?"

"No. I never beat her, and I've never beaten her. I'd never beat a woman."

"Then how do you explain the fact that she ran away 'for cover', as you put it, as soon as she saw you? Would she run for cover if she had had no previous experience of violence at your hands?"

"Perhaps she just felt guilty that I had caught them red-handed."

"And how do you explain that her medical report indicates that she had bruises and bumps on her face, consistent with wife battering?" Mr. Ngweshi produced a medical report as an exhibit for the court's information and record.

"That is for her to explain. I am sure she will tell the court where she harvested those bruises from, when her turn comes to testify."

"Now, Mr Liwetete, coming to the rape itself - can you tell the court what actually happened?"

"I want the court to know that there was never any rape. I tried to get my wife to explain what was going on between herself and her companion but she just cried. After a little while, one thing led to another, as they say on TV, until we found ourselves in bed, as man and wife. The rest, as they say, is history."

"Is it not true that she resisted and pleaded with you to stop forcing her to sleep with you?"

"She wriggled a little bit here and there, and said 'no please', softly and somewhat romantically. This is not unusual in African culture. In fact, our women are trained to show resistance before finally conceding. This is my experience, and all my friends share the same experience," Mr. Liwetete defended himself.

"So, you actually agree that you forced yourself on your wife?"

"No. What I am saying is that we did the things that men and their wives do under the circumstances which I have just described."

"My Lord, what Mr Liwetete has just described is rape, straight and simple. This court has proved, beyond reasonable doubt, that Mr Liwetete forced himself on his wife that evening. By his own admission, the accused has told this court that my client had said 'no, please' and wriggled hysterically to try to free herself, but he wouldn't have any of that. Instead, he subdued her, and raped her. I am terribly disturbed and dismayed by this man's animal-like and despicable behaviour. This man has no shame. I am completely sickened and nauseated by his disrespect for women; my large intestines are twisting, turning and twirling in disgust. I have no further questions for him."

In-as-much as the case for the prosecution revolved around the cross examination of Mr. Liwetete, the defence also based most of its arguments on the cross examination of Mrs. Mamunyandi Liwetete, whose cross examination by Mrs. Lubango was brief, sharp and to the point. This was conducted a week after Mr. Liwetete's cross examination.

"Mrs. Liwetete, do you recognise that man sitting over there?" Mrs. Lubango asked Mamunyandi while pointing to Mr. Liwetete – deliberately addressing her as Mrs. Liwetete to make her point.

"Yes," Mamunyandi replied.

"Can you tell the court who he is?"

"He is Mr. Liwetete."

"Is that all you can tell the court about him, don't you have any relationship with him?"

"He is my husband, but....."

"That is all the court wants to know and put on record. So, he is your husband, do you have any children with him?"

"Yes, madam, three."

"Will you be able to look after these children if your husband were to be sent to jail, possibly for a long, long time?"

"If it is in the interest of society and the law, I'll have no choice but to look after the children on my own," Mamunyandi stood her ground – having been as much as blackmailed by Mutokoya, her lover, to give this kind of response to ensure that Mr. Liwetete was locked up in jail, and the key thrown away.

"Do you know that you could also be sent to jail for a long time if you do not tell this court the truth, and no-one in this courtroom will be there to look after your children when both you and your husband are in jail..."

"Objection, my Lord! My learned friend is trying to induce undue fear and uncertainty in my client's mind. The defence is prejudicing the case," Mr Ngweshi interjected vehemently.

"Sustained! Will the defence counsel, please, restrict herself to the facts before the court," the judge ruled.

"I am sorry, my Lord. I just wanted Mrs Liwetete to regain her senses and realise the tragic consequences of her actions before it is too late. There are certain things one complains about in one's marriage, and others that one must accept and keep as an indispensable part of one's marriage contract. That's how we're trained as well-groomed and self-respecting African women. Even in Western norms marriage is ordained as a contract – a contract has responsibilities and liabilities."

"Objection, my Lord! The defence counsel is insulting the personal integrity of my client..."

"I am very sorry, my Lord, if my learned colleague feels that way, but that has never been my intention," Mrs Lubango cut in before the judge had a chance to make a ruling on the point of order, and she went on, "Now, Mrs. Liwetete, is it true that you slept with your husband on the day he found you unfaithfully entertaining another man in a house which belongs to both of you, please, answer Yes or No?" Mrs. Lubango demanded.

"Well, I didn't want to sleep with him...."

"My Lord, could you instruct the complainant to answer Yes or No. My question is simple: did she or didn't she sleep with her husband on the material day in question?"

"The witness is so instructed. Please, Mrs Liwetete answer the question accordingly," Judge Mulumesi ruled.

"Yes," Mamunyandi answered.

"In your earlier evidence to this court, you indicated that you slept with your husband against your will. Can you explain to this court how you made it known to your husband that you did not want to sleep with him at that particular time?"

"I wriggled and crossed my legs and told him to stop, but he persisted and forced my legs apart. This is when he began to beat me up. I was scared, especially because of what had happened earlier on," Mamunyandi lied. She was never beaten by Mr. Liwetete, on the day in question or on any day before that. Instead, it was her boyfriend, Mutokoya, who had beaten her up until she admitted that she had slept with her husband. Then he accused her of being unfaithful to him after she had earlier told him that she had long stopped seeing Mr. Liwetete, and that it was all over between the two of them.

"Do you know that people lose their lives, or become permanently maimed, due to unfaithful partners in a relationship, like yourself?" Mutokoya had retorted. It was subsequently his idea that Mamunyandi go to the police and report a case of rape against Mr. Liwetete. She was further instructed to include the beatings, inflicted by him, as part of the circumstances surrounding the rape. "If it is really true that he forced himself on you, why don't you go to the police station right now and report him?" Mutokoya had questioned her.

Under duress, and realising that her marriage to Mr. Liwetete was, for all intents and purposes, over, she surmised that securing her future with Mutokoya held better prospects than continuing to nurse spilt milk. At the back of her mind, she was hoping for a new marriage which appeared likely, especially if Mr. Liwetete were to be locked away in jail for a long time. She reasoned that with a previous conviction, there was quite a good chance of her version of the story being believed by the courts.

"What had happened earlier on, are you referring to your being unfaithful to your husband?" the defence attorney continued with her cross examination of Mamunyandi.

"Objection, my Lord!"

"Sustained! The witness will not be obliged to answer that last question."

"So, you slept with your husband, in your words, against your will. Was this the first time in the seven years of marriage that you slept with him but you were really not in the mood for sex?"

"Well, not quite. There were times when I slept with him but I didn't really want to have sex."

"So, you actually used to have sex with your husband against your will. Can you then tell the court what was materially different this time round?"

"It was different. I was not expecting to sleep with him. As a matter of fact, he was no longer staying at the house. It had been many months from the time he had moved out of the house to stay with his girlfriend."

"Can you remind this court what your name is?"

"Mamunyandi."

"Mamunyandi who?"

She looked around the courtroom hesitantly.

"The witness shall answer the question," the judge directed.

"Mamunyandi Liwetete."

"Open your eyes, Mrs. Liwetete! You're still my client's wife – now and on the day you slept with him after he caught you entertaining his best friend."

"On paper only - for all intents and purposes he isn't my husband anymore."

"Which intents and purposes are you referring to, and why are you still called Mrs. Liwetete?" Mrs. Lubango continued with her onslaught on Mamunyandi.

"I am just using the name because that is just the way it is - otherwise, there is really no marriage to speak about."

"Alright, I am sure the court has noted that you are my client's wife," the defence counsel summarised, "Now, let's go to something else. Are you aware that in African culture, a woman is expected to show physical resistance and say `no' principally as a way of being sexy and to excite her partner even more?"

"Yes, I know that but that happens at the beginning of a relationship. This relationship is at its tail-end."

"When you haven't been with your loved one for many months is it not like starting the romance all over again when he returns?" Mrs. Lubango pressed on. "Well as a fellow married woman, and as an experienced attorney in civil and criminal cases relating to marriage, I am putting it to you, and in fact assuring you, that there is nothing wrong or strange with what happened to you during these many other occasions you have mentioned when you had sex with your husband but you were not in the mood to do so. The same applies to what happened on the material day in question. It happens to all married women all the time. Our husbands have conjugal rights which they must exercise, more often than not, whether we like it or not. Besides, how was your husband supposed to know that on this particular occasion you really meant to deny him his rights?"

Turning to the judge, Mrs. Lubango concluded her cross examination, "My Lord, my client has no case to answer. With due respect, this lady has a double agenda. She is only trying to cover up for her unfaithfulness. What happened to her on the material day in question had happened to her many other times before. She must have had an ulterior motive for reporting the situation as rape this time around. As a matter of fact, what she described to this court happens to every married woman. Mrs Liwetete is being mischievous. She should be charged with defamation – defaming and shaming her husband publicly. She has not told this court the truth about the bruises and bumps that are cited in the medical report. She should be charged for perjury for lying under oath. I have no further question for her. She is an unreliable witness."

Unknown to most people, the issue of rape had a very personal significance to Mrs. Lubango. It was while she was in her final year at the University as a law student that she came face-to-face with the paradox of whether rape was an evil and undesirable thing, or not.

Over time she found herself being drawn by both invisible and invincible forces of attraction and love to the man who later became her husband. For over three years, she had been interacting with Mr. Lubango merely as a classmate, and as someone she worked with in the Christian association in which they both served on its executive committee. However, there was something different and mystical about Mr. Lubango – he was intelligent, humble and somewhat too reserved and saintly. At times he appeared to be somewhat troubled. In the more than three years that they had known each other, Mr. Lubango was not known to have had any girlfriend – nor did he appear to have had any intentions of having one. The thing that broke the ice between the two of them was a common task that they had to perform one day as committee members of the Christian association. They had been asked to preview and select a movie to show the next weekend. This was one way the association raised funds to run some of its community outreach projects. As they sat in this dark room watching the movies a divine spark involuntarily ignited their mutual feelings for each other. They started by holding hands, a little cuddle, and then each their first kiss – before Mr. Lubango suddenly got cold and froze. This puzzled his companion – Miss Ngw'elele Mu, as she was known at the time. Miss Mu had expected things to hot up, rather than go cold. "I must go," muttered Mr. Lubango, and he ran off unexpectedly – leaving Miss Mu unfulfilled and wondering what the meaning of all this was. "Was it something that she had said or done?" Miss Mu had silently asked herself in a mix of self-pity and genuine wonder.

Over the next little while, Mr. Lubango behaved rather shyly and awkwardly around Miss Mu. For her part, Miss Mu was unfazed by this confusion and knew deep down her heart that she had found a life partner. However, for the moment, she could not really make out what had gone wrong with the man she had known to be a near-saint in the years since their first year at university. "Perhaps it is guilt for a wrongly timed kiss," she consoled herself.

However, after a couple of weeks of this uncomfortable state of affairs, Miss Mu felt that this abnormal load was just too heavy to carry around. She found an opportunity to corner Mr. Lubango and went straight for the jugular, "I know that you're avoiding me, but I'll not apologise for that kiss. It was my first kiss, and I loved it. I'm not feeling guilty about it, and I do not care what you think."

Miss Mu expected some form of response or reaction from Mr. Lubango but got nothing.

"Today you're going to talk to me, whether you like it or not," she insisted. She went on, "I spend all this time with you because I like you, and somehow I know that you like me too."

On reflection, she began to feel cheap. As a well cultured African woman, she was not supposed to throw the first die, and declare her love for a man before he explicitly did so himself. She had surprised herself that she had gone as far as she did, and wondered whether it was university education that had disorientated and cheapened her morals, or just pangs of love pinching hard and mercilessly from inside her soul. For his part, Mr. Lubango just sat dumbfounded like a statue or zombie. Although he was not confused, his tongue was just too heavy to move.

This confrontation was taking place in Mr. Lubango's room. As a senior student he occupied a single room. This was the first time that Miss Mu had visited him there. She had invited herself after realising that from the fateful day of the spontaneous kiss Mr. Lubango was avoiding all occasion of the two of them finding themselves alone in a quiet place.

This was really a difficult situation for Mr. Lubango. He could not run away and leave her alone in his room, yet the longer she stayed the more uncomfortable he felt. He wanted her to leave and wished that she hadn't come. He did not even remember telling her his room number but realised that it wasn't difficult for her to have known this – after all, they studied together most of the time and his room number was visibly scribbled on all his books, in case one of them got lost. His room key would also be lying around carelessly as they worked together on numerous occasions.

"I wish you did not come to my room," Mr. Lubango finally heard his rude tongue blurt out.

"Too bad, I'm already here," Miss Mu was in a fighting mood and an uncompromising spirit.

"We do not even know each other well enough ..."

"Well enough for what?"

"I mean, you do not know me. You may think you know me, but you don't."

"Says who?"

Mr. Lubango was getting frustrated. Miss Mu appeared to have rehearsed this whole thing and it appeared that he had no strategy to counter her aggression and sense of purpose – whatever the purpose was.

"I always prayed that the first man I kiss will be my husband, and this is what will happen. So, if I were you, I would stop playing hard to catch. You cannot make me love you and then start playing hide and seek."

It was becoming quite clear to Mr. Lubango that Miss Mu's mind was running far ahead of his. She was now talking about marriage, just after one spontaneous and ill-timed kiss – not one that had been well planned in advance and well thought out; not even one that had been executed to its logical conclusion. It appeared quite frightening.

"Look, I do not want to spoil your life or be a bad husband. As a matter of fact, I do not even trust myself," Mr. Lubango was really in a tight corner.

"Well, I trust you."

"Please, don't. You do not even know where I come from, and who I am. I am not who you think I am."

"I may not know all these things, but I know who you are – my future husband."

"Please, just leave me alone. I have a very big family problem, and I love you too much to drag you into it – oh! I am sorry I said that 'love' stuff. Please, leave me to deal with my own problems. I do not want to make my problems your problems. I am talking about serious stuff."

"Who doesn't have family problems? We all have family problems and serious stuff. Just go ahead, shock me if you will. There is nothing that I haven't heard before," Miss Mu was unrelenting and feeling quite confident – inviting whatever Mr. Lubango could throw at her.

One of the community outreach projects that she was engaged in involved counselling young people in the church, as well as street children. So, she was convinced that the three years that she had been doing this volunteer work had prepared her for anything that Mr. Lubango would say.

"I am a son of a rapist. I do not know my father. I do not even feel like calling him my father. I have never called anyone 'father' – except for the priest."

"What?"

"I shall not repeat it, please leave me alone now! I do not deserve you, please, go!"

Miss Mu suddenly felt weak in the joints and bones. She felt dizzy and reached for the chair nearby. She was sweating and blacked out momentarily. Mr. Lubango panicked but still had the presence of mind to fetch some cold water from the bathroom and gave her a bit to drink – before laying her on the floor and pouring some of the water over her head, to shake her out of the possibility of a sudden death. She slowly regained her composure but could not utter a word.

Over the next few uncomfortable moments, they just stared at each other as if they both had no tongues. He then tidied her up; dried her hair and made her look as much the way she looked when she came in as possible.

After a little while, which seemed to Mr. Lubango to be an eternity, Miss Mu appeared to have sufficiently recovered, physically at least. Mr. Lubango led her out of the room and escorted her all the way to her room – all the while without anyone saying anything. Certainly, everything that needed to be said had been said. However, there was no second-guessing the fact that Mr. Lubango's visitor had been stricken by deep shock. Perhaps she needed counselling.

For his part, Mr. Lubango had known from a young age that the circumstances of his birth had been less noble than for the rest of the other children in the village where his mother lived. He was given a nickname which, literally translated, meant 'dirt' or 'rubbish'. The fact that he was the son of an unidentified rapist was a poorly kept secret in the village. It pained his mother, but not much could be done about it. The only relief came about when his grandmother came to get him at the age of twelve and put him through school out of the constant shame inflicted on him by the children and elders of the village in which his mother was married.

Over the next few weeks, it was Miss Mu's turn to avoid solitary contact with Mr. Lubango, as if to avoid being raped. For his part, Mr. Lubango felt relieved that his family secret was out, but wondered what Miss Mu would do with it. "Is she going to tell all her friends?"

The situation reminded him of the betrayal he suffered at the hands of someone he had considered to be his best friend at secondary school. He let him in on the secret, and the next thing he knew everyone in their class, and beyond, was talking about it. When he confronted the 'friend' he readily agreed that he told his friends because it was not his secret.

"It was your secret, not mine," was his casual and unrepentant answer. He went on, "If you could not keep your own secret yourself, how did you expect me to keep it?" Needless to say this was the end of the supposed friendship.

However, in the present case, Mrs. Lubango-to-be slowly brought herself back into the company of her future husband, still tongue-tied about the family secret. Without saying anything about the matter, the two young lovebirds grew inseparable, much like Siamese twins joined to the, you-know-what. The only visible scar from her husband's biological circumstances of conception appeared to be a missionary-type zeal that she exhibited in court cases involving rape – almost religiously defending those accused of rape. She behaved like someone who felt that rape was not such a bad thing, after all; that without it she would not have had a loving husband – humble as a saint and upright in every way; a husband who had given her two lovely sons and a very beautiful daughter. Certainly, her two sons did not look like future rapists. To the contrary, they looked as saintly as their father.

Mrs. Lubango never discussed the circumstances of her husband's conception with anyone, but every time she defended someone accused of rape her commitment and dedication to the case gave one the impression that acquittal was the only thing on her mind. One would even say she appeared to resent women who reported instances of rape.

<u>3</u>

Conscience is the inner voice that warns us somebody may be looking - H.L. Mencken, U.S. critic (1880-1956).

"Honey, won't you come to bed tonight?" Mrs. Mulumesi peeped through the slightly opened door of the judge's study. It was nearly mid-night and Judge Mulumesi was still working on his sentence for the following morning in the matter of Liwetete versus Liwetete. He was having a small problem with his conclusion, courtesy of his childhood friend Mr. Nembwe - a renowned and successful architect running his own consulting firm.

"Hey, look at the man who is about to send a fellow man to jail tomorrow for exercising his conjugal rights," Mr. Nembwe had teased his friend as he entered the bar at the country club.

Judge Mulumesi usually stopped over at the club for one or two on his way home, to cool off and clear his mind after a hard day's work. He drank sparingly and very responsibly – as if to live up to the public expectation – to remain 'as sober as a judge'.

Occasionally, he would drink himself silly – but only when he was at home and within a very close circle of friends.

In the heated discussion that followed Mr. Nembwe's opening remarks, everyone at the bar suggested that it would be foolhardy and dangerous to find Mr. Liwetete guilty – especially by a male judge.

"These things happen all the time, man!" remarked one man.

"Women like it when you use a little bit of force and exert your masculinity by flexing your muscles a little bit. They feel conquered, and they love it," remarked another.

"Gentlemen, the law is the law. If you don't like it, change it. If this is what you are doing in your homes, don't be surprised to find yourselves in my court one of these days - individually or collectively. The rotten days of male chauvinism are over - wake up!" retorted the judge.

However, it appeared that these remarks had some effect on him. After summarising the facts of the case clearly, he was finding it very difficult to find those nice words with which he could accurately and logically conclude the case. When his wife peeped and reminded him about going to bed, he heaved a sigh of relief.

"I've almost finished, honey. It is only the conclusion - one line or so. I can easily write it up tomorrow morning."

"Is it about this case everyone is talking about?" Mrs. Mulumesi enquired.

"Which case is everyone talking about?"

"The rape case – are you not handling it anymore?"

"Oh, yes. It is the one. Judgement is set for tomorrow morning."

"Tricky one, isn't it?"

"Not really. The facts speak for themselves," the judge assured his wife.

"It is not the facts people are concerned about. It is the principle people are looking at," Mrs. Mulumesi clarified.

"Which principle?"

"The question of whether or not a husband has to continue saying 'may I', 'may I', 'may I...' up to the end. What happens when the wife says 'no' all the time? What remedies does a husband get in the middle of the night and your court is closed?" Mrs. Mulumesi asked with an uneasy mix of humour and sarcasm in her voice.

"Well, as things stand at the moment it is hard luck. Besides, a judge cannot order a wife to have sex with her husband."

"Then you should not poke your nose in sensitive matters happening in other people's marriages – whether they come to you for relief or not. Send them back home to sort out their problems within their families," Mrs. Mulumesi thought she must have a final say on the matter.

The judge put his pens down; went to the bathroom to remove poison building up in his body – and then retired to bed.

Ironically, when the judge wanted to have his conjugal rights honoured later that night his wife declined.

"What is the matter, honey?" Judge Mulumesi asked his wife in utter frustration after several unsuccessful attempts.

"I am feeling rather tired today. Please, why don't you wait for the morning, I am sure I'll be feeling much better by then," Mrs. Mulumesi excused herself.

"Are you trying to prove a point here, honey?"

"What point?"

"This case you say everyone is talking about?"

"Oh, I was not even thinking of that. By the way, talking about that, I didn't hear you say, 'may I'?" the honourable lady teased her husband.

"Well, is it not obvious? When I start touching you in forbidden places, is it not obvious to you what is afoot?"

"Well, that is not what the law says. In fact, many wives are getting sensitised about their rights as a result of this case. Now I can recall the many times you actually raped me over the years; the many times when we had sex out of what I took as a sense of duty – an obligation, or as a compelling domestic chore which I had to endure. I even recall instances when I actually shouted to you to stop but you went ahead anyway. It did not occur to me then that you could have been sent to jail for that. The only problem is, who would have looked after our children had you been sent to jail? Anyway, I hope that in your administration of the law tomorrow you will do so wisely, and with due circumspection. I understand that the couple in question have young children who definitely still need to be looked after by both parents, whether or not they are staying together. If there is a score to be settled between the two parents, let this not adversely affect their children's futures. So, honey, whatever you have to say or do tomorrow, make sure that the children are protected under the law."

"Is that what the people are telling you? Now you sound like Mr. Nembwe. When I stopped over at the club this evening all the men were very worried about the outcome of this case. I am a servant of the law, and my duty is to interpret the law as it stands today. I should not be influenced by emotion or sentiment. I am sure I'll find my line in the morning."

"Honey, don't forget that this matter goes beyond the letter of the law. There is much more at stake and a certain level of wisdom, not just the knowledge of the law, will be required in your judgment. Don't sacrifice one man just to prove a point of law, nor should you jeopardise his children's futures for something that everyone does. You might just as well lock up all the men, married and unmarried, starting with yourself. You are a Christian and you know what the bible says: 'Don't try to remove a speck from your brother's eye when, Lo Behold, a beam is in thy own eye.'"

"Honey, for whatever your good intentions do not think that I have turned away from God. You know how much this house is governed by the word of God. I can remind you of other expressions in the bible which border on the same sentiments you are expressing – such as, for instance, the case of the prostitute when our Lord Jesus challenged anyone who regarded themselves to be without sin to cast the first stone. I am well informed in the ways of God my dear, and I am sure I'll get His guidance in the course of my judgement. He has guided and stuck with me all these years. He will not desert or forsake me now."

"Darling I am very proud of you. I suppose that finishes the argument. Your track record is quite impressive, and it more than speaks for itself. I am sure you'll not disappoint me in this present case. God is on your side."

4

*Do not remove a fly from your friend's forehead
with a hatchet* – Chinese proverb.

In the morning, Judge Mulumesi hurriedly
scribbled his conclusion and rushed off to work.

Before passing judgment, the Honourable Judge
Mulumesi called for closing arguments from both the
defence and prosecution.

"My Lord, we have to be extremely careful in
matters of this nature. It might even just be the case that
Mrs. Liwetete simply wants to get even with her
husband for deserting her for the number of months that
she claims he has been away. To say the least, her
motive for reporting this case to the police looks highly
suspicious. By her own admission, there were
previously many occasions when she was never
bothered by the sort of thing that happened on the
material day in question. She has failed to make it clear
to this court why she decided to call it rape this time –
and I am sure this is equally unclear to many more
people who have cared to follow her tale to the tail end
of this trial," Mrs. Lubango paused briefly before
concluding. "Besides, how can a husband know when

the wife really doesn't want to have sex and when she is just trying to appear dignified and sexy by teasing her husband and prolonging the foreplay? My Lord, there is no case of rape here. We are looking at two people in love; two people who share three children between them; two people who share a lot of history; two people who should be assisted to sort out one or two marital challenges which they may be facing, like most couples around the world do. Any decision or inclination to find my client guilty will set a terrible precedent. All husbands in this country will be so vulnerable they will dare not touch their wives; there will be no babies in this country, and this beautiful nation will soon become extinct before we all know it. For any man who will dare be adventurous and touch his wife awkwardly, the consequences and repercussions will be deadly, grave and severe – leading to an unprecedented upsurge in civil and criminal cases by vindictive wives and girlfriends against their innocent husbands and boyfriends. Our courts will have no time to hear any other cases apart from these frivolous claims coming from disgruntled and vengeful women."

As Mrs. Lubango finished her closing argument, many in the audience were nodding their heads in agreement.

The judge gave the attorney for the complainant his time to make his concluding remarks.

"My Lord, this is a straightforward case of rape – simple, unambiguous and clear," Mr. Ngweshi began to speak. "The law clearly states that any man who exacts sex out of a woman against her will commits rape. The law does not make any distinction based on the nature of the relationship between the offender and the victim. They could be total strangers or they could be husband and wife - it is as simple and straightforward as that."

Mr Ngweshi looked around the courtroom as if to gauge the extent of support and approval he had in the audience for what he was saying. The court was silent, everyone looking down, avoiding eye contact with the prosecutor. Most of the people thought his line of argument was rather academic and far removed from reality - whatever the law said. He continued, "My Lord, by his own admission, Mr Liwetete has told this court that my client wriggled, cried out, screamed, pleaded and fought to free herself from the defendant. She shouted 'no', but the so-called husband ...."

"Objection, my Lord! Mr Liwetete is not Mrs. Liwetete's 'so-called husband'. It is in the records of this court that Mrs. Liwetete is Mr. Liwetete's legally wedded wife," Mrs. Lubango corrected her learned friend.

"Sustained! The relationship between Mr. and Mrs. Liwetete has not been contested in this court so far," ruled the honourable judge.

"My apologies, my Lord! I withdraw that statement," Mr Ngweshi apologised and continued with his argument. "As I was saying, my client wriggled, fought and did all she could to free herself but that man sitting there wouldn't have any of it. He still continued to use his masculine, muscular power, subdued my client and forced himself on her. My client crossed her legs and held them tight, but the defendant forcefully disentangled them and forced her to have sex with him. He showed the highest possible level of insensitivity and brutality. She was sexually assaulted and suffered excruciating physical pain. This is naked brutality and gender-based violence at its worst – utter selfishness.

This man was vicious and a typical wild animal," the prosecutor paused briefly before continuing. "The defence has not refuted any of the material evidence presented before this court. My Lord, this is a clear case of rape and, as such, I urge you to find the defendant guilty, as charged. Let me also remind the court that the defendant has had a previous conviction for the same offence. No man should ever construe raping women, taking it as a desirable hobby or habit. Clearly, this man has taken this despicable act for a hobby. He thrives on violence against women, and that is totally unacceptable in a civilised society like ours. Accordingly, this court will be failing in its duty if this man were not found guilty and was let loose on society. The prosecution recommends that he be handed the maximum sentence possible under our laws for this crime. Letting him free to roam our streets and neighbourhoods will be tantamount to giving him further opportunity to unleash his libido on unsuspecting innocent women in our country; our daughters, our sisters and our wives will not be safe. By affording him further opportunities and ammunition to hurt more and more women, more encouragement will also be given to others with similar tendencies to do the same with impunity. I have nothing further to add – this man disgusts me in the absolute sense. Society needs to be protected from people like him; he requires and deserves the severest punishment possible."

After the concluding remarks from the two attorneys, the packed court fell silent as Judge Mulumesi sifted through his papers to put them in order to deliver his judgment. When he was finally ready, Judge Mulumesi began to read his pre-written summary of the case:

"That husbands and wives have conjugal rights over each other in a marriage is not the issue before this court. The issue is how this right is exercised and what the law says in this regard. Courts do not formulate laws. Those who have problems with the letter and essence of the law as it stands today should see their legislators to have it amended, or changed," he paused for a brief moment, looked around the courtroom like a land surveyor, and then proceeded. "Let me remind all of you here present, that these are not courts of justice but courts of law. Accordingly, you should realise that courts do not administer justice but we merely interpret the law and offer protection to the public and innocent victims in terms of the prescriptions of the law of the land - no matter how unjust it may appear to some of you..."

As the judge went through his judgement, Mr. Liwetete sat silently with his head hanging low and heavy between the palms of his hands. After what had happened to him previously, he was well aware that, sometimes, the heavy and wide bum of the law crushes innocent people. His mind wandered back to his dark days in prison - the hostilities among groups of inmates, the food, the work routines, the prison warders, the various unorthodox ways to cope with the natural sex drives and cravings, the shame of being in prison - and above all, the wasted time: day by day, one's life just rots away and nobody outside seems to care, or even notice.

When you are in jail on a long term sentence, time just comes to a stand-still: there is no present, no past and no future – you're just there. You are not sure whether you are alive or dead. For now, it looked as if the nine years he had innocently spent behind bars had been for nothing. His life had come full circle from the days of Nembele to today. "Is it not enough that a man is sent to jail for nine years for a crime that did not exist?" his mind wanted to know. He wondered what the maximum sentence would be this time round, after today's conviction – particularly considering that he was now to be regarded as a repeat offender and habitual criminal. It was really a fight against history. He was well aware that in the official records of the country's judicial system, he carried a previous conviction for rape, which stood unchallenged. He had wanted to launch an appeal against the Nembele conviction after he came out of prison, but just felt so bad about the wasted years and his damaged reputation that he decided to 'let sleeping dogs lie'. Now, sitting here and listening to the judge telling him what he already knew, made him wonder whether he had done the right thing by not challenging the previous conviction. "I hope that the honourable judge will realise that in this particular case it is me who is the rape victim, not my wife," Mr. Liwetete consoled himself, hoping against hope for a miracle judgment in his favour. The dream, or rather nightmare, that he had the previous night did nothing to help matters, either. In the dream, it was a dark night – pitch black outside. The sky hung low, under the weight of gloomy and ugly clouds, interrupted only by lightening and thunder; fuelled by strong winds blowing from the North-East. It was a frightening night as trees and the tall grass around his house shook and whistled melancholic songs of the underworld. Then the skies suddenly opened up and everyone was happy to be out on the streets – and there he was: running stark naked in the streets under the full glare of everyone, in broad daylight. He was being chased by a lion, but he was unable to run fast. As he tried to flee to safety he kept falling down, as if heavy lead was tied to his ankles. He would then wake up abruptly in the nick of time just as the lion was about to pounce on him. Every time he fell asleep, the same dream kept coming back – and, each time he woke up, he wondered what the meaning of the dream was – and why it kept coming back. But for now, his mind went back to what Judge Mulumesi was saying.

"... The court has heard how Mr Liwetete mercilessly disentangled his wife's legs, almost breaking them at the knees, while she was shouting to him to stop ..."

As Judge Mulumesi summarised the evidence put before the court, Mr. Liwetete was suddenly gripped by an uneasy combination of fear and grief. The problem was that this particular judge had a bad history when it came to cases of rape. A few moths previously, he had presided over a case that everyone thought was a waste of time to even have eaten away the precious time of the judiciary system.

"There are so many awaiting-trial criminals in this country – I mean, real criminals, but they're tying up the court's time prosecuting an innocent man!" remarked one man.

This was after a Tonga man had been convicted and sentenced to a mandatory three-year jail term – without an option of a fine, following a brief affair he had had with a Chewa woman. The Chewa woman reported the Tonga man to the police after she found out that the man was not from the same tribal grouping as herself.

"I had made it very clear to this man that I could only have an affair with, or get married to, a man from Eastern Province, where I come from. Repeatedly, this man lied to me that he was also from the same tribal cluster. He even gave me a false name – that he was Mr. Zigzag Phiri. I would never have slept with him if he had told me the truth that he was a Tonga man from Southern Province. As soon as I found out I immediately rushed to the police station to report the matter. I felt naked and violated. In fact, his real name turned out to be Kingsize Haabasimbi," the woman had testified.

The police charged the man with 'rape by deception' and Judge Mulumesi found the man guilty, as charged. The man's only line of defence was that he loved the woman dearly, and he would have done anything to win her over. Furthermore, he informed Judge Mulumesi's court that he did not know that falling in love with a Chewa woman was a criminal offence in the laws of the country. Certainly, he had never imagined that loving a woman and treating her well would ever have ended up being construed as a crime.

"This court is not saying that a Tonga man cannot fall in love with a Chewa woman," Judge Mulumesi had explained. "Neither is the court saying that a Tonga man cannot marry a Chewa woman – after all, this is a free country. The charge put against the defendant is that knowing full well that the plaintiff would not have agreed to having an affair with him, he elicited a relationship with her – for the purpose of having sex with her, by misrepresenting himself. As such, he slept with her against her will. I am afraid I have to find the defendant guilty of 'rape by deception'," he had concluded.

Women rights organisations were divided over the judgment – some welcomed it, while others weren't quite convinced it was the right thing to do. Some even thought a mere warning would have been enough. A sizeable proportion of detribalised women were outraged. Needless to say most men were horrified by

Kingsize's conviction. One male observer saw it as follows:

"Perhaps Judge Mulumesi was trying to be funny. Well, we have to tell him that this is far from being funny; we fail to see the joke in his assertions and actions. The country condemns him for his inability to be funny, and for his total lack of a sense of humour. We call for his immediate dismissal."

Another man retorted, "I'll never understand why every time there is a misunderstanding between a man and a woman, they charge the man with rape. Why did they not charge this man with 'fraud' or 'impersonation' – or something like that?" the man took it so personally that he was even failing to breathe properly as he spoke. He concluded, "At this rate, very soon men will not be allowed to look at women – they'll call it 'rape by looking'."

In the light of Kingsize's recent mishap with the law, it was not hard to understand why Mr. Liwetete kept on blinking away tears of anticipated grief, as he listened to Judge Mulumesi summing up his judgment. From the way the judge was twisting and exaggerating the evidence in favour of the prosecution, it was becoming clearer and clearer that a conviction was imminent – perhaps just a few seconds away. He imagined the prison doors opening – and shutting behind him, and some of the long-term jailbirds recognising him as one of their own; perhaps even asking him taunting questions like, "We missed you, what took you so long?" or passing comments like "We knew you would be back. This place is so nice that nobody comes here only once – once here, you have to come back again."

As Mr. Liwetete's attention drifted back to the judgment, he was already resigned to any eventuality. He felt vulnerable, exposed and ready for the judicial hungry vulture, called Judge Mulumesi, to rip him apart – even before his last breath had been used up. Metaphysically, and even as he sat waiting to hear the now all familiar rhetoric of 'guilty', he felt that his blood was being sucked up by the legalistic vampire sitting at the bench to his righthand side, wearing a woolly white headgear, in hot weather.

As he sat there, many uncoordinated thoughts raced through his mind. He wondered whether it wouldn't just be easy on the mind to simply accept the reality that he was, once again, destined for prison. Still, he had difficulty countenancing the thought that he had really done anything wrong – so wrong that the wrong he had committed could only be fixed or repaired by him going to jail, yet again. Casting his mind forward, he started to think that perhaps he needed to commit a dreadful crime upon his second release from prison, just to get even with the judicial system. This way, he would compensate for all the wrong time that he would have spent in jail – either for no crime at all, or just on frivolous grounds. For now, though, he was not able to wrap his mind around a dreadful enough crime which would enable him find peace and closure, once he had committed it. Neither was he able to confirm to himself that he was actually cut out to committing crimes dreadful in the extreme. For the moment, the one crime, dreadful or otherwise, that appeared to be permanently plastered to his name was the one of rape. He was probably a rapist, after all.

He had now grown to have mixed feelings about courts. Before he was sentenced the first time, he used to think the courts were places where you went for relief and justice, to be liberated from people of evil deeds and the ill-intentioned. Some people even assured him before the day of his conviction that a court of law was like a woman's womb – which exuded love to the unborn baby, dutifully served him/her, sheltered, supported and nurtured him/her, and above all, protected and shielded him/her from the evil elements outside. This way, you would agree that you're really presumed innocent until proven guilty. As it was, he felt that he was presumed guilty from the very first day he entered the police station – all the way to the first day he had walked into the front door of this revered courtroom. As his mind wandered back to the judgment, he could not help but also reflect on this particular judge's meanness of spirit. The judge was moving towards his conclusion:

"Further evidence of what happened that evening included a medical report which confirmed penetration and that the sperm found in Mrs. Liwetete's body belonged to her estranged husband," the judge went on.

"The question regarding African culture and tradition and, therefore, the involuntary nature of sex between husband and wife within the African context..."

Judge Mulumesi paused and looked at Mr. and Mrs. Liwetete, in turn. He reflected on what his wife had said the previous night; the uproar and horror that had seized the Zambian society following the last rape conviction and sentence he meted out to the overzealous and deceptive Tonga man who masqueraded as an honourable Chewa gentleman. His mind also wandered to the biblical prostitute and the challenge Jesus gave to the crowd; he remembered the comments made at the country club by his childhood friend, Mr. Nembwe, and others. He glanced at the two attorneys.

"I cannot decide this case. Please, find another judge," Judge Mulumesi hammered his gavel with a deafening thud as a signal to mark the end of all proceedings, and left hurriedly for his chambers. On a matter of conscience, he could not proceed with his pre-prepared judgment.

"My Lord ...!" the prosecutor protested as the judge disappeared to the back of the court room, leaving the court in utter confusion and bewilderment. He rushed to the toilet, tore up the papers and flushed his judgment down the municipal plumbing system.

www.ingramcontent.com/pod-product-compliance
Lightning Source LLC
Chambersburg PA
CBHW030515130626
46549CB00007B/3002